Rogue

Stephanie Bedwell-Grime

Rogue

Cover Art by Derek Grime

Published by Feral Martian Publishing

ISBN # 978-0-9917590-9-5

ROGUE

Wind drilled sand against my windows. I paused, a mug of *stim* halfway to my lips, looked through the pressure-sealed glass and sighed.

This is my life now, I thought darkly. I get up. I shower. I switch the cats.

The cats' roar greeted me as soon as I stepped into the enclosure. Desert Lahti aren't what you'd call sociable. They don't even care for the company of their own species. Still, I have limited space here on my small patch, so I've been trying to spread their scent around in the vain hope that they might learn to tolerate each other. They don't know it yet, but those two are going to mate. I was feeling especially doubtful about that whole enterprise as the scaled desert cats sniffed each other disdainfully, snorting at each other's scents, and hissing at each other through the mesh fence. I eyed them with some annoyance. Did no one in my life ever get along? They loathed each other almost as much as my mother had hated my late BetaaDon boyfriend, Yaub. Which, I suppose, was understandable. Mom was the Admiral, and Yaub was an alien. Even coming from an allied planet didn't make him suitable boyfriend or Heavens forbid, marriage material.

So I was a little surprised to see them both peering over my compound fence watching the snarling Lahti nervously. I blinked in shock. Mom and I hadn't been on speaking terms for some time. Not since I'd retired from the air force. And Yaub was, well...dead. I blinked again, focused. Memories flooded in, I choked them back.

On second glance, the guy with my mom wasn't Yaub. Still, he looked enough like him to be his twin in a bald, blue-skinned kind of way. Yaub had been taller, broader in the shoulders. I swallowed past the lump in my throat. Yaub had been my lover and my best friend.

I came to my senses suddenly, realizing I'd left them to stand in the glare of the three noon-day suns. Just because Mom and I had disagreed about Yaub–oh hells, we'd disagreed about everything–was no reason to be rude.

"Come around to the gate," I called.

They hesitated, cast another glance at the growling Lahti. Even the BetaaDon seemed to have a healthy fear of them. Hells, I had a healthy fear of them.

"The cage is locked." When they still didn't move, I added, "And fortified."

They moved as one then, coming around to the gate. I keyed in the sequence to drop the force field, let them through, then reset it.

I noted they stayed as far away from the Lahti cages as possible. I glanced at the BetaaDon. He stared back at me with yellow eyes, so like Yaub's it made my breath catch.

"Let's go into the house. It's climate controlled."

The fourth planet out from the blazing suns was even hotter than my home world. Growing up I'd loved the relentless heat. Years on climate-controlled ships thinned my blood more than I cared to admit. Being back in the home system, I was becoming acclimatized once again, but just barely.

I led the way into the house, letting the sudden blast of cool air chill my skin. No one had said anything yet. I didn't want to start another war with my mom by saying the wrong thing, so I waited.

The uncomfortable silence stretched. She could have called, I thought angrily, then let it go.

I motioned for them to follow me into the cramped kitchen. I still had that pot of stim brewing. I picked up the pot, shrugged my upper shoulders in question.

"Andromeda," my mother began interrupting me mid-shrug. "This is YaubRux."

Shock hit before memory kicked in. BetaaDon put their family names first. I'd mistakenly begun calling Yaub by his last name before I'd realized that. Good naturedly he'd let me and the nickname stuck. His first name had been Lal, but I'd never called him that.

Rux, Rux, the name circled around in my brain. Then realization hit. Yaub had family in the military. Rux was his cousin. Older cousin. The family resemblance was remarkable. I dragged my thoughts back to what I remembered about Yaub's family. Last I'd heard, Rux had been posted to the BetaaDon Home World Defense Force in our war against the Zenians. Apparently now he was hanging out with my mom. That couldn't be good.

Abruptly, I became aware that I was standing there with the stim pot still in my hand and I hadn't said a word. I shoved my lower right hand out. Not really proper protocol. TriiYonites always shook with their upper right hands, but that would mean juggling the pot or turning my back to him to put the pot down, which would be even ruder.

Rux didn't seem to notice. He shook hands. He had a firm grip, I noted. “Lal's cousin,” I said. He nodded.

“My daughter Andromeda,” my mother said. Like Rux didn't already know that. My liaison with Yaub had been legendary. We’d been the first inter-species couple. Or at least the first publicly inter-species couple. But not the last. Either way, Mom wouldn't be forgetting that. Not only had I not done her proud in the military, I hadn't made a decent marriage alliance either.

“Stim would be nice,” Rux said, breaking the silence He had a pleasantly deep voice that reverberated down my spine. Like Yaub's had.

I turned to get more mugs in an effort to distract myself from that disturbing thought.

“Not for me,” my mother said. Mom had no vices. None I knew of anyway. I filled Rux's mug, grateful for something to do. “So,” I asked turning back to them and handing Rux the steaming mug. “What brings you here?”

Mom looked suddenly bashful. I swallowed, wondering what could possibly be bad enough to bring my mother out to the planet she openly called a wasted expanse of sand and rock.

"Actually…" Rux said. He spoke passable TriiYonite. It sounded vaguely exotic in that resonant voice. Warm fingers brushed mine as he reached for the mug.

I wouldn't, couldn't think of that, I told myself. Yaub was gone. Rux bore a striking resemblance to his cousin, but he wasn't Yaub.

My mother followed my embarrassed glance. Her lips thinned in displeasure, kind of like the Lahti, I mused. But then, she blurted, "We've come to ask for your help."

My gaze flickered from Rux back to my mom. "My help?" I squeaked.

Mom looked unfazed. One thing I knew for certain, the admiral didn't beg. "Yes."

One word and she expected the favor would be granted. No explaining and absolutely no begging. It wasn't that she wouldn't if necessary. It was just that after a lifetime of being in charge, the thought never occurred to her.

Still staring at her, I swallowed hard. “In a military kind of way?” I made sure my voice didn't squeak this time.

“Perhaps.”

Rux was watching us carefully, a hint of amusement just barely tilting his lips upward. If I wasn’t used to BetaaDon company, I wouldn't even have caught the gesture.

“Okay,” I said. I might as well agree to it. Didn’t matter if I'd heard the specifics, if Mom asked, I was expected to do it. “Could you perhaps give me a few more details?”

Rux's golden eyes darted from the admiral back to me. “Forces are gathering on the edge of BetaaDon space.”

Oh great. That was a big help. “Military forces?”

“Perhaps.”

I felt Rux's eyes on me, waiting. I couldn’t really tell, but it looked like he wanted me to agree to whatever it was. I turned back to my mom. "Forgive me, but what has this got to do with me?"

My mother sighed. For the millionth time I felt like I wasn't the successor she had hoped for. It was an old grief, and I put it aside. "You have the most experience with inter-species relations," she said, with extra emphasis on the *relations*.

I really didn't want to go there. How many times did we have to fight over Yaub? Especially now that he was long gone. I pushed the thought from my mind. I had briefly been the Zenian ambassador. And I'd lived with Yaub openly for years. In xenophobic TriiYonite society that made me an expert. Great. Just great.

"And you think it might be the Zenians?" I asked. Why else would the BetaaDon want me to intervene on their behalf? They had their own ambassadors. None, however, that had been effective in dealing with the Zenians.

"It might be the Zenians," my mom admitted, "but we don't know for sure. The equipment they've been using is unfamiliar to us."

Which meant it probably wasn't the Zenians. While they'd put a brave face during the generations-old war with us and the BetaaDon, it hadn't been evident until the war was over, how dearly it had cost them. Zenians just didn't have the resources for more aggression so soon. Unless, of course, they'd found new allies.

“But I can't just pick up and leave,” I protested, knowing before I spoke my objections would make little difference. I waved my arms at the expanse of desert outside my kitchen window. “I have a ranch to attend to. I just can't leave the Lahti so close to breeding season.”

“Didn't look like they were too keen on it,” Rux said, the first words he'd spoken in the conversation.

Well, thanks a bunch. I gave him a sour look. To which he looked immediately chastened.

“They're always like that,” I said. “Breeding Lahti is a bloody business.”

Rux looked relieved. What on earth had Yaub told him about me? “A bit like war,” he volunteered.

That made me laugh. “Kind of like.”

“The air force is prepared to provide a caregiver for the ranch,” the Admiral said, spitting the word like a curse, “and the Lahti.”

Which of course, left me no room to maneuver. “I haven't seen combat in years,” I protested. “I haven't even been in the cockpit of a ship!”

“The military is also prepared to provide remedial training.”

“Remedial–” I'd been one of the best pilots in the air force. If you ignored the collateral damage.

“You shouldn't need much,” Mom said pointedly. “It's primarily a recon mission.”

Primarily. One couldn't be too careful when talking to my mom. I sincerely hoped she didn't expect me to come back dead. I echoed her sigh. “Well, since the arrangements are all made, when and where do I report?”

She nodded to Rux. “YaubRux will brief you. I expect you at the barracks on BetaaDon Prime tomorrow.”

Unexpectedly generous of her. At least I'd get a couple of hours sleep. I opened my mouth to thank her for that small mercy, but she'd already swept from the kitchen and out into the blinding heat. I hoped Rux had his own transport.

Silence settled in the cramped confines of my kitchen. Outside I heard the female Lahti issue a warning growl to the male. I doubted whatever caretaker the military provided would get them to mate. So much for next year's herd. I sat down heavily in my chair. Rux took the seat across from me.

“You aren't like your mother,” he observed with the same understated dry humor I remembered Yaub having.

“No.” I stared into the depths of my forgotten cup of stim. “I'm sure not.”

He smiled then, his expression heartbreakingly like his cousin's. “A relief that is.”

I grinned back, ignoring the error in his grammar. Unlike Yaub he obviously hadn't spent that much time in the TriiYon system. “So...” I settled back in my chair, resigned to hours of briefing, followed by hours of hunting for my old uniform, followed by hours in transit. I desperately hoped I could find the uniform, that it wasn't too worn and that it still fit. I really didn't want to turn up in the barracks in civvies. I could just imagine the look on my mother's face now. No, I'd find the uniform, run it through the sanitary and squeeze it into it somehow. Failure was not tolerated in my family. I'd go to the edge of BetaaDon space whether I wanted to or not, just because Mother had asked. I gave Rux the full weight of my stare, which could be like Mom's if I was in a bad enough mood. “What have you got?”

Surprisingly, it was pretty much like Mom had told me. Unidentified ships were gathering at the edge of BetaaDon space. They hadn't answered any of the coalition’s hails. A team was being assembled to venture out there and hopefully make peaceful contact. *Peaceful* being the operative word. The war had been tough on both us and the BetaaDon. Another war would pretty much sink the interstellar economy.

Rux, it seemed, had been left as my personal escort. Like Mom expected me to try and escape. I guess maybe she thought I might. I'd retired. It could hardly be considered desertion, but Mom obviously had some stake in this. Apparently, she didn't want any incidents.

Yaub's cousin had brought his own dinner. Maybe Yaub had told him about my ineptitude in the kitchen. I was no cook, by either TriiYonite or BetaaDon standards. It if didn't come pre-packaged, dehydrated or cooked by someone else, I didn't eat it. The BetaaDon was already tearing into his dinner while I reheated last night's leftovers. Maybe he was just worried about the difference in BetaaDon and TriiYonite diets. BetaaDon could tolerate most of what we considered edible, yet there were a few of our foods that could make them sick. After living with Yaub, I'd learned to stock only things we could both eat. Since he'd been gone, I'd gotten out of that habit. So it was probably wise of Rux to provide for himself.

My small house came with a climate-controlled guest room, so I guess Mom had just assumed I'd put him up for the night. Shaking my head, I went in search of that uniform.

I found it in a box of things I'd meant to toss in the recycler. Luckily I hadn't gotten around to it. Wouldn't have wanted to try and explain that to the Admiral. Even more surprising was that it was still reasonably clean and free of blood stains. I remembered what had happened to its predecessor and winced. It did however smell musty, so I tossed it in the sanitary. Now all I had to do was worry about what to do with the BetaaDon still sitting in my kitchen.

For a moment we stared at each other uncomfortably. I'd thought perhaps Yaub's family had been more comfortable with our inter-species union than mine. He rarely said anything about it. Or perhaps it was just rude by BetaaDon standards to comment on private matters. They were kind of uptight that way. Still, by the way Rux was fidgeting nervously, I suspected he was feeling uncomfortable with the whole thing. The troublemaker side of my personality contemplated seeing just how uncomfortable I could make him. After all, I was out of sorts. I didn't want to venture to the edge of BetaaDon space, leaving my home and my livelihood behind. Taking it out on someone else had a distinct appeal. In the end I took pity on him. He was probably just as much of a hostage in this as I was. And he was Yaub's cousin. After all we'd shared, I owed Yaub's family some courtesy.

"I had planned to take a short nap before we leave." I pointed down the hall to the tiny office that doubled as a guest room. Not that I had many guests. "If you want to do the same, I have a place where you could–"

"Yes," he quickly agreed, cutting me off. "Sleep would be welcome. Doubt we'll be getting much once the mission begins."

"You're coming with us, then?"

"Us?" He looked confused to a moment. His TriiYonite wasn't as good as Yaub's, but it was better than my very rusty BetaaDon.

"Our recon team," I clarified.

Rux fell silent a moment, searching for the right words. "I believe the two of us comprise the team," he said very formally.

I said, "Oh."

Being forced back into duty and sent to the edges of charted space was one thing. Being locked up with Yaub's cousin for the gods knew how long quite another. He did seem like a decent sort, but that decency came loaded with memories and regrets. I didn't need any more of either.

Maturity must have been working its hand on me because instead of all the things I could have said, instead of all the injustices I could have railed against, I said merely, "Come, let me show you where the guest room is."

I left him sitting on the fold-down bed in my office, while I wandered down the hall to my own room, to probably the last water shower I'd have in a very long time and the last comfortable bed I might ever lie in.

After a short nap, I pulled the old uniform out of the sanitary, texted Mom the house's security code and left the Lahti an extra-large helping of food and water. Hopefully, the promised caretaker would arrive before the Lahti ate each other and my ranch fell to ruin.

Rux emerged from his nap looking annoyingly refreshed. Just as I was about to ask him how exactly we were getting to the BetaaDon base, I heard the roar of a small ship landing. It seemed our escort had arrived.

I waited until the dust had settled, then I shouldered my pack, armed the security system and followed Rux out into the blinding sun to begin my second involuntary tour in the air force.

The barracks on Beta Prime was cramped and cold. I'd found the relentless TriiYonite suns difficult to get used to again, but the damp and the cold on Prime was even worse. I'd accompanied Yaub on a couple of visits to the BetaaDon home planet. I'd met some of his family. Part of me admired their innate politeness and restraint. Part of me felt suffocated by it. In any case it was a long time ago. After all that had happened since then, I'd forgotten how bone numbingly cold the wind around the base could feel.

Remedial training turned out to be a standard hour in a virtual flight simulator and a tour of the cramped cockpit of the new BetaaDon craft. I hoped the caretaker the air force had arranged for my ranch got more consideration, but I doubted it. I wouldn't be living well next year, I mused. If I survived whatever the military had in mind for me.

BetaaDon technology had really come along since I'd last set foot in one of their ships. Then again, TriiYonite tech likely had, too. I really hadn't kept up. Fate it seemed, conspired to get me back in action. Or maybe it was just that the Admiral couldn't bear the thought of her only child becoming a Lahti herder. Really, I should have known.

An hour later, stuffed into the cockpit of a BetaaDon two-person recon ship, I found myself heading for the edge of charted space. It's a good thing I slept in transit, I thought, glancing over at Rux sitting close enough for me to smell what he'd eaten for lunch. The craft wasn't built for four-armed beings. I'd always found BetaaDon accommodations cramped for that reason. I folded my lower arms across my stomach and glanced at my companion. What he thought of the whole scenario he didn't say. For the millionth time I cursed BetaaDon reticence, then gave up. It made sense to send a BetaaDon since the aliens were gathering on the edge of their territory. What didn't make sense was what I was doing in the equation. It couldn't be all about my mother's dislike for my new occupation.

I let Rux take the lead, I could read BetaaDon, knew the basic outlay of their ships. I let him input coordinates and followed his orders, even though I outranked him. Or at least I had. My acquiescence seemed to make him nervous.

After about a hundred of his solicitous head-bobs, my patience snapped. “Why me?” I asked out loud.

My outburst startled him. “I don't understand,” he said, hedging, sensing my anger. If he was in league with my mother on this, I'd rip his head off, Yaub's cousin or not.

“Sure you do,” I insisted. No way was I letting him off the hook by feigning issues with language or culture. Lal had won far too many arguments that way. Until, of course, I'd caught on to his strategy. “Why am I on this mission? I haven't been in active duty for years. I'm not BetaaDon. I'm not...what you need,” I finished lamely.

Rux looked acutely uncomfortable. “I requested your presence,” he said suddenly.

“You! Why?”

“Lal thought highly of you.”

“Yeah, well Lal and I were–”

He held up a hand for mercy. “Please, I really don't want to know.”

So the BetaaDon weren't any more liberal when it came to inter-species relationships than their TriiYonite counterparts. They were just quieter about it.

"Fine," I agreed. No sense torturing the guy. "But did it ever occur to you that Lal might have been, well...biased?"

"No," he said surprisingly. "When it came to military matters, Lal was of his own mind."

That much was true. Once YaubLal made up his mind, there wasn't any way of changing it. What I'd never understood was how much of his mind had been taken up by me. He'd been openly critical of my cavalier ways. My outspokenness had grated on his nerves. That he'd been secretly proud of me was a revelation.

"Okay, but what if I can't do what you want me to do? What if I'm not capable?"

"I do not doubt your capability," Rux said, eyes firmly on the control panel. "Lal used to say your mind worked in ways no one else's did."

That made me laugh. I could just imagine what else Yaub might have said. “And you think that might help in a First Contact situation?”

“I sincerely hope so,” he said, sounding so remarkably like Yaub it brought tears to my eyes.

“Great,” I said, turning away. “Just great.” I swallowed, sniffed back the tears and looked squarely at him. “Well, YaubRux, I think we're screwed.”

To that he laughed out loud. My outburst didn't shock him. On the subject of me, he'd been well briefed. “No, Andromeda Spar, I think we'll be just fine.”

I would have felt better about his assurances if I wasn’t the one who was supposed to make it so.

I tracked our progress on Rux's instrument panels. Icons flashed by on the screen, marking our progress past the twelfth planet in the BetaaDon system. Once we passed the last station and mining outpost, the traffic grew more sparse and the chatter via in-system communications less frequent. I'd been out here before, of course. I'd been most places in charted space. Our war with the Zenians had been brutal and far-reaching. Already I was longing for the relentless glare of my home planet's suns, the scrape of blowing sand against the windward wall of my house and the occasional growls of the Lahti. I glanced over at Rux. He didn't seem inclined to idle conversation. BetaaDon never were. We TriiYonites were far more garrulous, a trait that had driven Yaub crazy. Especially because I'd often done it on purpose. Maybe it hadn't made him as crazy as he'd let on, I suddenly thought. Maybe he didn't get along with his own kind anymore than I did.

We reached the dark space between BetaaDon and TriiYonite territory and the section that bordered on Zenian holdings. Many of us had been sent this way. Few had returned. I'd had the unfortunate experience of being a guest in a Zenian detention centre. Twice. I didn't want to go back.

I kept my eye on the screens, looking for anything that might seem unusual. Kind of difficult since I had no idea exactly what to expect.

“There!” Rux said abruptly, making me jump.

I glanced at the screen, still seeing nothing out of the ordinary. “Where?”

He pointed to a dark shape on the screen, one I'd taken for a shadow against the rapidly diminishing spec of the BetaaDon home star. Long past the edges of the BetaaDon system, I hadn't expected to find anything so big out here. With no light to reflect, it was hard to spot. Yet, there it was.

“A rogue planet?”

Rux nodded.

“But surely, if you'd had a rogue world out here so close to your system, you would have mapped it by now.”

He looked pleased that I'd given the BetaaDon the benefit of the doubt. TriiYonites are notoriously bigoted.

“So, it couldn't have been here before,” I said, following the train of logic. “It had to have been moved.”

“Exactly.”

"Do you think the Zenians have the tech to do such a thing?"

"No way to know. Our intelligence hasn't picked up anything that might indicate such a jump in their technological ability."

"Unless the Zenians have been hanging out with a new race since the war ended," I mused. A frightening enough prospect in itself.

I leaned on my lower arms and reached out with my upper right hand to trace a path from where I knew Zenian space began. The trajectory just didn't seem right. Not that that meant anything significant. Who knew where the Zenians had found this strange feral planet, if in fact they had.

"Okay. Assuming the Zenians have made some new friends. Ones with tech far beyond our wildest imaginings..." It sounded even worse when I said it out loud. "What possible reason could they have for parking a whole planet just outside your solar system?"

"I shudder to think," Rux said.

"But wait a minute! I thought you said you'd discovered ships out here."

Rux pointed to the screen. Just as I'd spoken, I noticed a flurry of activity around our ghost world. "Oh, no."

Rux merely nodded. "You see the problem."

I leaned in for a closer look, resting my upper arms on the console and keeping my lower set folded beneath it. An uncomfortable position at best. That was the problem with being forced into close quarters with another species. I always felt cramped and desperately afraid that if I so much as moved a muscle, I'd knock something over.

My discomfort was soon forgotten as I stared at the flurry of moving dots on the view screen. "Can we magnify that further?" I asked, again afraid to reach with the wrong set of hands and punch in the wrong codes.

Rux pointed out the appropriate buttons. I zoomed in, the picture enlarged. Dots became entire ships. Ships like nothing I'd ever seen. "They look..." Finding no TriiYonite term, I struggled to find the right word in BetaaDon.

"Crustacean?" Rux supplied.

"That's it!" No wonder the word eluded me. Coming from a desert planet, we had no corresponding type of wildlife. I studied the image. Those ships did look like the underwater creatures Rux suggested. I'd seen files of such things. BetaaDon ate them. The thought made my stomach turn. But then, Yaub had found the thought of eating Lahti quite repulsive. Different species, different tastes, different planets, cultures.... Sometimes it all made my head spin.

Many species based their machine design on their biology. Having four arms, TriiYonites tended to arrange things in groups of four instead of the customary BetaaDon two. Still, what possible function could crustacean-like ships have swarming around a rouge world out in the middle of nowhere? And how did a planet all alone out in the void support life anyway?

Technically speaking, I knew it was possible. It had been awhile since I'd studied science, not since the academy. Still, I thought I remembered something like–if a planet had been kicked out of its solar system early in its development, it might still be enveloped in enough hydrogen to keep heat from escaping and possibly allow for liquid water. It seemed far-fetched, yet there it sat, dead ahead of us.

Of course both the TriiYonites and the BetaaDon were expecting us to unravel the mysteries of this strange, cold world. Lucky us.

I sighed. Rux glanced at me in askance. "We're just going to have to get closer."

"Agreed, but how? They're going to spot this ship for certain."

Supposedly we were flying a reconnaissance craft, but still I had to ask. "Weapons?"

"We have them, but our fire power is negligible."

"Great."

Rux said nothing.

I glanced again at the odd-looking ship on the screen. “So somehow we're going to have to isolate one of their ships, then.”

“All right...” From the look on his face, I could tell Rux suspected I'd taken leave of my senses. Probably I had. “That is one possible course of action.”

“I'm open to other suggestions.”

He spread his hands. “Regrettably, I have none. We need to examine those ships up close. We need to know who is flying them. We need to know what they intend so close to BetaaDon space. And we dare not come any closer in our obviously alien craft.”

“Record as much information as you can while we're here,” I said. “Then we'll move out of range, watch where they're heading and lie in wait for one of them to cross our path.” That maneuver was a basic Lahti hunting strategy, I couldn't help thinking with dark humor. So I had learned something from my time as a Lahti rancher after all.

I watched as Rux assembled his files. Shots of the ships from every angle we could see flickered across the screen. We filled more databanks with details of the rouge world as well.

I studied the feral planet. “I'm guessing that if we could get close enough, we'd find it pretty cold and dark.” I thought of how eerie the surface must be out here in the void with no sun to warm it. Did creatures that mimicked those strange ships exist in its frigid seas? Were the ships perhaps some kind of bio-tech monstrosities grown in their dark depths? Just the thought of those black oceans made me shiver and long for the glare of my home system’s suns and the relentless hiss of shifting sand. I really, really, really didn't want to get any closer to that dark wilderness.

“We have to consider that it might have a hydrogen atmosphere that acts as an insulator,” Rux suggested, apparently thinking the same as I had.

“Volcanic activity might also keep it warm,” I added. “Well, warmer.”

"Warmer being relative." Now that was a very Yaub thing to say. I was getting used to the similarities between Yaub and his cousin. Each glance and turn of phrase no longer made my heart ache.

We captured every detail we could at that distance and drifted back to wait. If those were scout ships, some of them ought to come scouting at some point. Rux had the helm. There was nothing to do but scan and wait. Lack of sleep caught up with me. I let my eyes drift shut. I'd spent countless shifts this way, waiting for orders, waiting for something to happen.

Abrupt movement dragged me from the depths of what had to be a sound sleep. I jerked awake. My lower arms hit the bottom of the console. I felt the engines kick in, then the drives come on-line.

Not only had I developed the ability to sleep upright in uniform, but I'd also learned to wake up quickly. "What do we have?" I asked.

By the chrono on the console, I'd only been asleep for one standard hour. Rux obviously hadn't. He looked like he could have used a nap as well. "Movement," he answered.

He already had the guns–whatever meager weapons the ship had–online. I mirrored his actions, finding the appropriate controls on my own console. On the view screen I watched a blip cut across the space in front of us.

A scout, apparently on the move. At least I hoped it was a scout, not some alien equivalent of a munitions ship. If it was, I reflected darkly, I likely wouldn't have long to worry about it.

Rux trailed them at a distance. Adrenaline flooded my system. I hated battle, really I did, despite the fact that I'd made it my career. But I did enjoy the hunt. The rush of vitality hit my veins like a potent drug. They said warriors got addicted to it. I believed that. Still, I wasn't addicted. I could go back to Lahti ranching any day.

I could. No matter what my mother said.

Oh really? A quiet voice inside asked. I ignored it. Lahti rancher or no, whether I wanted to be or not, I was in the midst of battle. Or about to be anyway.

The scout left the company of his fellows and headed out into the dark. We followed, inching closer. I glanced at Rux. His jaw tightened. Didn't look like he enjoyed battle any more than I did. The scout had seen us now. He picked up the pace. We zoomed in closer, trying to cut him off.

Rux was a competent pilot, but our quarry was getting away on us. "Give me the helm." It came out way more like an order than I'd intended. I expected him to object, to remind me that I was an observer and there only to help if necessary. But he keyed in a few commands and my control panel came online.

I swung both sets of arms up on the console. My brain was meant to operate both sets of arms simultaneously. Watching Rux had been painfully slow. The BetaaDon equipment felt confining. Rux would have to duck if any of my elbows got in his way, but it felt great to be able to do what my body was designed to do.

I input new commands, forcing my brain to remember how it felt to operate the BetaaDon craft. We swung around. I gave full control to the thrusters, pulling power from every other source expect life support. A risky move. Still, we wanted this guy. If in fact he was a guy. Who knew what kind of creature piloted the alien craft. We gained on him. He tried to evade us, but I was the better pilot.

I rerouted power to what weapons the craft had and fired on what I hoped was the alien's weapons battery. If I guessed wrong the consequences could be deadly. For us.

The alien ship bucked. Looked like I'd hit something vital. Maybe I’d whacked their weapons array, or possibly their propulsion drive because now the ship lay unmoving in space and we were sliding into it far too quickly.

“Brace for impact!” I yelled.

I sent power to the reverse thrusters just in time, saving us from a bigger impact than I'd feared. Still the crash sent us flying against the webbing of our harnesses.

“Cameras?” I asked Rux. He blinked once, then keyed in some commands. The exterior cameras came back online.

I glanced at the image on the monitor. The crustacean-like ship drifted beside us. We'd left a blackened hole in its side. Ice crystals congealed around the fissure as its atmosphere escaped. So at least they breathed...something. Chances were if whoever was inside was still alive they'd be pissed with me now.

“Does this ship have any kind of in-space docking equipment?” Damn fine time to ask, I realized belatedly. What Rux thought of my way of doing things, he wasn't giving any sign.

With relief he nodded.

“How about breathers and contamination suits designed for TriiYonite physiology?”

Another nod. I guessed he still felt shaken from the impact and getting slammed against the inside of the harness. My own bruised ribs complained, but I had no time to see to my injuries. Nothing felt broken.

I sucked in a deep breath. Big mistake by the pain those bruises inflicted. “Okay.” My own voice sounded as strained as I felt. “Let's go see what we've got.”

I headed down the docking tube, a flexible, clear, insubstantial structure that unnervingly showed the stars around us. I focused on the hole we’d blown in the alien ship, afraid to look up or down. Or anywhere else for that matter. Fervently, I wished for the metal, utilitarian docking tubes the TriiYonites used. There was something comforting about the opaque tubes. This clear thing didn't even look strong enough to hold my weight. But, I reflected darkly, it was easily detachable. That made me nervous. Rux was still on the BetaaDon ship. One of us had to stay in case of emergency. One of us had to be in control should things get nasty. Since I had more experience with alien contact that meant I was the one elected to head into the dark and the cold. And the one who'd be abandoned there if things didn't go our way.

Hardly the first suicide mission I'd been sent on, however it was the first in awhile. I was out of practice.

The hole loomed before me. I stopped thinking about the clear, vertigo-inducing tube around me and headed for it. Whatever substance the ship was made of, it didn't look like metal. Doubtful that anyone inside understood either TriiYonite or Standard, but I yelled in both languages over my suit radio. “Allied forces! Open up!”

Predictably, there was no response.

I might be out of practice, but some of my warrior instincts had kicked in because I came bearing four guns. I drew two of them, the first in my upper right hand and the second in my lower left. I wasn't as good a shot with either of my lefts, but I wanted one right hand free for combat.

I yelled again in Standard. Still no answer. That didn't necessarily mean anything. There could be an entire army waiting inside. In which case things might go very badly for me.

Well, I decided, if an army lurked on the other side of that door, they were well aware of my presence now.

I flattened myself against the side of the ship. No bolts of energy came flying through that hole to greet me. I took that as a good sign.

I blasted another bolt of energy inside. Still no movement. Hesitantly, I stepped through the fissure, both guns still drawn. Hardly a friendly way to greet a new race, but no way was I going in there unarmed.

Atmosphere thick like fog swirled around me. The hiss of my suit's ventilations system sounded loud in my ears.

"Okay, I'm in," I said over the suit radio.

"Acknowledged," came Rux's crackling reply.

"Are you recording?" I asked Rux over my suit radio.

"Recording everything," he answered. A warning—maybe. I couldn't be sure.

I ventured down what I assumed had to be a hallway. Though not like any I'd ever seen. The ceiling curved down to meet the floor and the corridor curved back on itself at so many points it made me dizzy. I pointed the light on my helmet in every direction, trying to capture as much as I could for our files, but I couldn't shake the feeling that I'd been swallowed in the belly of a great beast.

That metaphor struck me so suddenly, I stopped.

"Something wrong?" came Rux's query.

"No," I answered. "But I had a thought."

Yaub would have added a comment to that, something like, 'will wonders never cease?' I missed his biting sarcasm, his running commentary on the universe according to YaubLal.

Rux, being far more reserved, said nothing. I made myself remember he was a separate person, enough like his cousin to cause me odd moments of sentimentality, but still a separate being with his own habits and his own thoughts.

I kept my head steady as I walked toward a nearby wall. Reaching out a hand, I pressed it into the strange, pliable substance that covered it. It didn't feel like metal, or wood, or any material I could name. I pressed harder.

The craft shuddered, tossing me backward onto my butt. It heaved again under my weight, like trying to choke me out.

“What is it?” I heard Rux's voice, but the constant heaving and tossing made it difficult to answer. “What's happening?”

“Not sure,” I said. “But I think it's trying to get rid of us.”

“Get rid of us, how?”

Damn the BetaaDon tendency to be literal.

“I think it's trying to throw off your ship. And to choke me out!”

“But if it were trying to throw me off and choke you out of its system, then that would mean it was–”

“Alive,” I finished for him.

“Sentient,” he supplied simultaneously.

“Right.”

So much for first contact. Instead of introducing ourselves politely we'd blasted our way into a sentient being and were now roaming around in its belly. If in fact it had one.

Gods! My mother was going to love this one. I could just imagine what she'd have to say about the way I'd botched the mission for both her and the BetaaDon in whose territory those ships were lingering.

“If it were sentient, it should have tried to communicate with us.” Now Rux was actually sounding a lot like his cousin.

“Maybe it didn't know how.”

“It obviously belongs to a space faring society,” he pointed out, like that explained it all.

“Maybe it can't talk now that we've blasted a hole in its skin and I'm walking around inside it.”

“A reasonable hypothesis,” he conceded.

“So what now?”

"Now we try to talk to it."

"Great, just great. How in hells am I supposed to talk to it from the inside?"

Thankfully, he didn't say 'well, you're the first contact expert, you figure it out.'

That didn't change the fact that I was the alien contact expert and they were expecting me to figure it out—whether I wanted to or not. Now that I was inside, I did have to find a way to communicate with it from its interior. Hopefully, without killing it. That would most probably be seen as an act of aggression. At least I'd consider it an act of aggression.

"I'm going to move further inside," I told Rux after a moment. "Maybe there's a way to communicate with it."

"Understood," Rux said. His silence told me what he thought about my chances of actually having a conversation.

"At least perhaps we'll have a better idea of what we're dealing with here."

Or so I hoped.

I moved off down the corridor. I forced myself to think of it as a hallway. If I started thinking of it as the inside of some creature's guts, as its air passage or its circulatory system, I might be sick. So I continued down the winding access way, trying to tread carefully and cause as little damage as possible.

The hallway had to be part of its respiratory system, I decided, judging by the fog that rolled past me in gauzy waves. It made me hold my breath for a moment, even though green lights still show on the inside of my helmet, telling me my suit's ventilation system still operated correctly. Taking a probe from the pack at my waist, I took some samples of the fog and moved on.

I couldn't be causing the creature that much distress because I didn't feel any more heaving underfoot. At least that's what I hoped. I didn't want to hurt it. I'd given up killing when I left the air force. I'd done my share of it before. Nightmares still haunted my sleep, but after years of herding Lahti, they'd been getting less frequent. Until the

Admiral showed up and destroyed the peaceful life I'd built for myself.

"Still reading me?" I asked Rux. BetaaDon weren't prone to small talk or aimless conversation. I missed that camaraderie. Especially while I trudged through the guts of a semi-sentient, space-faring creature on the edges of BetaaDon space.

"Reading you," Rux confirmed. "Though your signal is weak."

Great. The last thing I wanted was to get lost in the belly of that thing.

"Okay, then. If this is its respiratory system, I'm going to go looking for its brain."

Rux replied something that sounded like the affirmative. I turned and headed down the far hallway. If I could find the brain, I reasoned, I could try and communicate with it. Assuming that was possible from the inside. Who knew? No one had ever encountered something like this. Lucky me.

The blast hit me from out of nowhere. I fell, skidding onto my hands, two of my guns going flying. I watched in horror as a mucous-like membrane seeped from the floor. My guns disappeared into it.

Pushing myself up with one palm, I tightened my grip on my two remaining guns. Mucous smeared my palm. I felt grateful for my suit's thick gloves and hoped whatever it contained couldn't penetrate them. I'd be spending a long time in decontam if I made it back alive.

“Andromeda?” came Rux's worried hail.

“Got a bit of trouble,” I said and turned to face what had flattened me to the floor.

The corridor seemed empty. Or so I thought until a nearly colorless tube-shaped entity bashed me again. The impact left a smear of something gooey on my suit. I had a second to think, *yuck!* Then it hit me again.

Instinct took over. I got my guns in place and fired.

It reared back before rushing at me again.

I cursed. My guns fired before I even realized I'd pulled the trigger. So much for worrying I'd lost the reflexes. Apparently, they still worked just fine.

With a whoosh, the thing collapsed like a flaccid balloon. I fired again, just in case. The whole ship bucked under the impact. Briefly, I thought of getting out my pack and taking a sample while it writhed on the floor, but before I could put the thought into action, that mucous stuff congealed around it and it disappeared.

"Captain Spar?" Rux's voice.

"Here," I answered. "I think I just might have met its immune system."

A long silence ensued, then, "Status?"

"Still alive to tell the tale."

"Repeat?"

Again I wished BetaaDon came hardwired with better senses of humor.

"Continuing my prior course," I clarified. "Heading for its brain. Oh, and by the way, I'm running a little short on artillery."

Another pause. I guessed Rux found my sense of humor as baffling as I found his. "Do you wish to return?"

"Not yet. I still have two guns with nearly full charges. I'll see what else I can find."

And then we were going to high-tail it back to TriiYonite space and I was going to go back to being a Lahti rancher.

Whatever damage we'd done to the ship must have been repairing itself because at that moment, the ship took a sudden dive. At least it felt like a dive from inside. I felt the motion through the floor, the walls. Deep down in the bowels of the ship, I heard a humming sound start up. Momentum increased, tossing me into the far wall.

I scrambled to my feet, afraid if I rested anywhere for more than a moment I'd get sucked into that goo that had eaten my guns.

"Andromeda?" came Rux's panicked hail.

"Here," I answered. "What's going on out there?"

"You're moving," the BetaaDon said.

"Guess we didn't damage their propulsion, after all."

"Apparently we did not."

“No kidding.” I prayed we had hit their weapons array instead as I’d first thought, as I raced back down the corridor hoping to reach some kind of brain or communication center before our momentum tore Rux's ship apart.

“I'm going to have to disengage the docking tube,” Rux said, obviously thinking the same thing.

A stab of panic tightened my stomach. The last thing I wanted was to be marooned alone in the belly of the beast.

“Can you follow us?” I asked trying not to sound as frightened as I felt.

I felt the creature shudder as the docking tube was disengaged. I tried not to remember how our guns had blasted a hole in its side.

“Pursuing.” The BetaaDon sounded strained. “My flight models estimate its trajectory as heading back to the rogue world.

“No, no, no!” I chanted to no one in particular.

“I didn't catch that,” Rux said, then something intelligible. “We might be out of radio contact for a while,” he finished.

“Promise me you won't leave me here,” I radioed back, wincing at how forlorn and pitiful I sounded. The radio went dead. I couldn't tell whether Rux had heard my reply or not.

So this is how it ends, I thought darkly. After my less than stellar career in the air force, after facing my retirement and the fact that nothing more interesting than Lahti ranching might ever happen to me, I was destined to be digested by some unknown creature on the fringes of BetaaDon space. My mother would be horrified. Luckily, I wouldn't be around to see it.

Around me the ship bucked and shook, as if trying to expel me from inside, or perhaps trying to vomit me back into space. I kept racing down the corridor toward that junction where the hallways branched off. I had to find a way to communicate with it, or at the very least to find a way to turn it around back in the direction of Rux and my ticket back to civilization.

I arrived at the junction and peered down the tunnel. The corridor twisted and turned so much I couldn't see much except the next bend.

Now that the creature seemed back on its course to the rogue world, its bucking and shaking had stopped, but I could still hear the humming coming from deep inside.

I bolted down the hallway, running as fast as I could in the curving corridors. We were still moving, that much I could tell. I could feel the motion through the floor beneath me. I kept trying to reach Rux over my helmet radio, but all I got was a sputter of static.

Finally, the tunnel belched me into another curved room, one vastly different than the last. I skidded to a stop.

Now, I had only a passing knowledge of biology, even my own, but it seemed to me that the giant tubes branching out of the bulbous thing in the center of that room might be veins. I glanced again at the structure. Pale and round, it pulsed with blue light from within. I drew closer. It looked like something moved under the surface. Not light, I realized, but a blue substance moving through a netting of tiny veins beneath the pale skin. Those tiny veins branched into larger tubes as they exited the round fleshy structure, which in turn disappeared into the floors and the walls like highways heading off in all directions.

Was this its brain? How could I tell? And even worse, how was I going to communicate with it?

"Rux?" I asked just in case. No one answered.

Oh, this was just getting better and better. It might not matter if I could communicate with it or not. If it kept moving out of range, I might never make it back to TriiYonite space.

Just as I was thinking that dark thought, I felt an increase in motion. I lurched forward, skidding into that brain-like structure. My hands, the ones without the guns met something pliable. Through my gloves I couldn't tell if it felt warm, but it did feel soft. Surely its brain would have some kind of hard protective case. It did, I realized. It had a hard outer shell, which we had blasted a hole in. I was probably the first being ever to walk around inside one of these things. Lucky me.

I tried to lever myself away from the thing, but the motion increased until I was hanging nearly face down, pressed against it. The creature was diving, I realized, probably down into one of those frigid seas on the rogue planet. I had to find a way to communicate with it, to convince it to turn around and head back into open space and let me go.

The momentum eased up enough that I could push myself up by my two free hands. As I did I noticed something in the depths of that translucent bulb. Images, foggy and indistinct swirled before my eyes. I increased the magnification on my helmet and looked again.

The rogue world loomed within the milky depths. No mistaking that eerie dark place. It grew, nearly filling my vision. My heart kicked once at the inside of my chest. My hands tightened on my guns, even though I knew weapons were useless here. I didn't, really, really didn't want to go there. Would Rux follow me? Or would he adhere to BetaaDon protocol and return to base while they endlessly discussed tactical possibilities?

We were moving even faster now. While being inside the creature protected me somewhat from the g-force, I could still sense momentum. The vision of the rogue grew in the optics of this strange bio-engineered ship. It occurred to me that I was looking out from the inside of whatever constituted its eyes. By the size of the image rushing up to meet us, I assumed I'd soon be getting a guided tour of that feral planet.

We broke through the insubstantial atmosphere, still diving. Having no other thing to brace myself against, I shoved out my arms, the tips of my two empty hands lightly touching the brain. Even though I knew they were useless, I still wasn't willing to give up my guns.

Falling toward the rocky ground, I expected a bone-jarring crash. Or perhaps even a bone-shattering impact, but instead we plunged into freezing liquid. Our trajectory evened out. I drew in a shallow breath and stood up.

Not sure what to do, I aimed my guns at the brain. Hardly diplomacy, and surely not the best way to begin first contact, but hey, I was a trained warrior, what did they expect?

I almost did shoot. Really, I didn't want to dive any further beneath those frigid seas, perhaps never to see the surface again. I didn't want to slowly suffocate in the bowels of this strange creature. Still, I didn't want to shoot it, either. I'd already shot my way inside it, traveled its guts in ignorance thinking it was like the ships I was used to, hard, metal things without feeling or consciousness. Now I hovered inside its brain like a virus. No wonder it wanted to go home to nurse its wounds.

Suddenly, it occurred to me that if I could see in, perhaps it could see me. Hesitantly, I holstered my two remaining weapons and crept closer, my four hands raised in the universal posture of surrender. Would it understand?

As I watched, the pictures within the sphere changed. I could still see the murky dark sea reflected on the back of what I supposed had to act as its retina. Superimposed over the picture of that cold ocean was my own image. Then the pictures changed. The shift in perspective made me dizzy. It took me a moment to realize it was showing me some kind of playback. A memory perhaps. With nauseating clarity, I watched as it showed our ship blasting a hole in the craft, and then my clumsy descent into its bowels, followed by the attack on its immune system. I watched again as the mucous swelled again and stole my guns. Then I saw myself charging down those tunnels into its brain.

The image paused there, waiting. Without language, how could I say sorry?

I wracked my brain, trying to think of how to make a connection. Moving slowly, I took off my holsters and lay them down on the floor of the chamber. I half expected them to disappear into the membrane, but they didn't. Okay, so it understood my intention to talk peacefully somehow.

I had no way of communicating visually, except for the handheld computer clipped to my belt, and I couldn't think of any way to provide a suitable interface.

Then it occurred to me. The handheld could take handwritten input. Used to make notes, it was crude in the extreme. I was no artist, but it was all I had left. I didn't want to stay here beneath the frigid seas of a feral world, trapped inside an alien creature.

Slowly, I unclipped the handheld from my belt. Hesitantly, I held it up, afraid it might misinterpret my actions and think it was a weapon. It seemed to be waiting to see what I'd do, so with the stylus I quickly sketched what I wanted to portray. Under my hand a crude representation of the BetaaDon system appeared. I added the TriiYonite system and then sketched stick figures to represent the two-armed BetaaDon and us four-armed TriiYonites.

I held up the tiny screen and waited.

A new image appeared within the sphere, a reasonable likeness of the rogue world drifting alone in space. A flurry of organic ships dotted the skies around it. Okay, so we'd established where we came from. Now, how to ask what they wanted here?

I drew another picture. This one included the BetaaDon system, plus the rogue world. I held it up to the sphere and shrugged all four shoulders.

It responded by displaying a similar image.

But what did it mean? I had the sneaking suspicion it meant they intended to stay here out on the fringes of BetaaDon space in possible striking distance of the TriiYonite system as well. I doubted that was going to go over well with either the TriiYonites or the BetaaDon. How was I going to ask it if its intentions were peaceful?

I pointed to the guns lying on the deck and hoped I hadn't just made an aggressive move.

It responded by replaying the image of my guns disappearing into the floor. Did that mean it was going to oppose any aggression on my part, or that it didn't agree with violence? I drew a picture of the alien ships and added a representation of my guns.

It responded with an image of the creatures minus the guns.

I guessed that meant their intentions were peaceful. I thought of the consequences if I'd misunderstood. Did it understand the concept of lying? How could I possibly know?

I decided its intentions wouldn't matter if I suffocated here. So, I drew another picture. This one showed me, all suited up with four arms standing on the shores of the sea alone. Then I added a crude representation of the creature disappearing back into the watery depths. Like I said, I'm no artist, but I held it up to the sphere and prayed to long forgotten TriiYonite gods that I could make it understand.

For a moment nothing happened. Now, I thought, I'm going to find out that it can lie, that it's been lying all along and I'm going to bottom of that icy sea never to be seen or heard from again. Thoughts of all the things I'd miss rose unbidden. An image of Rux flashed into my mind. Even though we hadn't known each other very long, I'd miss him. Strangely, I found myself thinking of my mother, wishing I'd taken more time to mend things between us. Did she ever think of me that way? Every time I'd gotten myself shot up, did she worry? Did she wish she'd left things differently between us?

Movement shocked me out of my reverie. We were climbing, I realized with relief.

The ship rose for what seemed like a long time. Then our trajectory seemed to even out. I felt a thud and struggled to keep my feet.

Around me a giant wind began to blow. I clipped the handheld back on my belt and reached for the sphere to try and steady myself. But the breeze picked me up, suit and all and tossed me back down the hallway like I was no more than a piece of paper. I bounced off walls, ceilings and floors as I careened back down the corridors, until finally I came to what looked like a puckered aperture. It dilated and I was blown free.

The impact jarred every bone in my body. For a moment I lay where I'd fallen, content simply to breathe, grateful my suit's apparatus was still operational.

Beneath me I felt hard ground. Cold enough to penetrate even the skin of the suit, it felt like it had been frozen forever. I looked up and saw a scattering of diamond-edged stars above.

A giant crash shook the ground. I turned just in time to see the giant creature slide back into the frigid sea. Ice jutted around it. Chunks of it closed above its head as it disappeared beneath the surface. A splash of something wet crested the rocky shoreline. I scrambled hastily out of the way and looked around.

I stood on a rocky precipice looking down into an icy sea. What the liquid was composed of, I didn't know. I wasn't sure at this point I wanted to get close enough to take any more samples. Leave that to the scientists and the discovery team. I'd made contact. We'd talked in a fashion. It was up to the BetaaDon and TriiYonite governments to decide if they wanted this rogue planet and its strange inhabitants sitting on the edge of their home systems.

I just wanted to go home.

Glancing up, I studied the inky black skies. Nothing moved. Nothing that could be easily distinguished as Rux's ship. I activated my suit radio.

"Captain Spar, here. Requesting immediate pick up!"

Static. And then, "Andromeda?"

Relief washed over me, followed quickly by exhaustion. I had no idea how much time had passed in the guts of that thing. My stomach growled as loudly as a Lahti.

"Rux," I answered. "Get me the hells out of here!"

***

After that things happened fairly quickly. Rux, along with a multitude of TriiYonite and BetaaDon air force ships, swooped down to rescue me from the rogue world. Guess my mother, the Admiral, wanted me back more than I'd thought. I arrived back at the BetaaDon base only a little worse for wear, which was in far better condition that the last few times I'd been rescued. The samples I'd taken, along with my handheld, and the crude drawings I'd made were confiscated. Diplomatic proceedings began.

The rogue world now sits at the edge of BetaaDon space, far enough out of the solar system as to not be too much of a bother. Turns out the inhabitants don't like the sun much.

I'm currently on leave and awaiting clearance to return to TriiYon Delta. The military doesn't want to let me too far out of their sight...for now. I shudder to think about what kind of shape my ranch is in. Apparently, the custodians were successful in getting the Lahti to breed and I now have a litter of kittens. It's going to be a busy summer. If, in fact, they let me go home.

Now I'm trapped on the BetaaDon home world in barracks that don't conform to my TriiYonite physiology. It's only a matter of time before I break something. Hopefully, nothing too valuable.

Rux has offered me a place to stay. I don't know whether to take him up on it. I like Rux, but there are just too many memories there. He reminds me far too much of his cousin.

So here I am, the proverbial fish out of water. Not that I've ever seen such a thing. On BetaaDon I have more in common with the inhabitants of the feral world. I don't belong in either world. I guess that's what made me so valuable to the army. I've always been an outsider even among my own kind.

Maybe I'll visit the rogue world, once diplomatic relations are more firmly established. After all, I owe one of its inhabitants a big apology.

ABOUT THE AUTHOR

Stephanie Bedwell-Grime is the author of more than twenty novels and novellas and over fifty short stories. She has been nominated for the Aurora Award five times and has also been an EPIC eBook Award finalist. Stephanie welcomes visitors to her website at www.feralmartian.com.

20991424R00041

Printed in Great Britain
by Amazon